Expressions
for the Lover of
My Soul

Expressions for the Lover of My Soul

Hazel O. Kersellius

Table of Contents

Prayer of Gratitude

"Blessed are they which do hunger and thirst after righteousness: for they shall be filled." Matthew 5:6 KJV

Dear God,

I give glory and honor to you, my Creator, my God, from whom all of my blessings flow. I give you all the glory for the great things you have done, continue to do, and will do in my life. I enjoy delighting in your presence and seeking your face above all else. I thank you, God for showing yourself faithful even when I have fallen short so many times. My joy is in you, Lord. I am so grateful.

Thank you for comforting, counseling, encouraging, and correcting me in your unconditional love. I appreciate you for showing yourself mighty in my life. You have proven yourself over and over, time and time again.

Thank you, dear God for infusing me with this wonderful gift of writing. Thank you, Holy Spirit who led me to the discovery of my gifts. Thank you for my passion for you, Christ the Lord, which unlocked my desire to express my love for you so freely. Thank you for giving me the inspiration for this poetry.

God, only you know my beginning and my ending. You are faithful to complete the good work you started in me. For that, I remain grateful.

Your child,

Hazel

Acknowledgements

I would like to thank my family, friends, mentors, noted ministers, and church family for your love and support. My late grandparents, late Uncle Hilton, late Aunt Roxanne and late Aunt Hazel would be so proud of me. Their love lives on.

A dearest thank you to Fred M. Brown for standing by my side, and who is to be an author of many books. Thank you for your love, support, prayers, words of encouragement and poetry that continues to minister to me on a personal level and to so many others. You are such a blessing to the body of Christ.

Special thanks and honor to my late Bishop Everett C. Newsome and late First Lady Olga Newsome, the founders of my home church, Saint Albans Gospel Assembly.

Special honor to my leaders, Apostle Everett C. Newsome Jr. and Apostle Marjorie Newsome, for pouring into me sound biblical teaching with a wealth of knowledge and wisdom of God's Word. Thank you for building me up in the faith and encouraging me during challenging times. Thank you for encouraging me to develop a relationship with God through Christ Jesus for myself. It has been, and still is, a joyful journey that can be difficult at times, but you helped me see that this walk is bigger than me. As unpredictable as it is, the rewards in God far outweigh the obstacles. Along the way I have no regrets because I know it is not in vain. It is worth every step to embrace my process as I focus on the promises of God. Through my personal relationship with God, there is a confidence I have in Him that will not be undone.

Thank you, Saint Albans Gospel Assembly family, for your love, the heart you have behind what you do, and for your passionate prayers, fellowship, care, support and allowing me to bless you with what God has given me to minister. For all those who took the time to hear what God has placed on my heart, thank you for listening and for your feedback, especially when I would get so excited like a kid in a candy store—bursting with the desire to share my poetic works with you as it would come fresh off the press. I have a warm appreciation for you individually and collectively.

Special thank you, dear Apostle Claudette McIntosh for your all of your care, love, fellowship, prayers and encouragement over the years, and to the House of Shiloh. Each of you have helped me strive for greater in many ways. I appreciate all you've shared with me.

Thank you, Pastor Sandra Manning, Associate Pastor and Elder Sheryl Joe, members of Dabar Bethel Cathedral. Thank you, Pastor Sapphire Jackson and Mrs. Valerie Grimes, (author) of Restoration House of Power for allowing me to share with your ministry what God has given me. I appreciate you for being a part of my humble beginnings that were not despised but very encouraging in my journey.

Great honor to the late Pastor Michael D. Samuels of Empowered Prayer Teaching Prayer Line for his heart for encouraging me to get this book out in the last stretch of publishing, and for the heart he had for seeing God's people excel in excellence for the Kingdom of God.

Special thanks to my mentor, Apostle Marjorie Newsome for your love, great wisdom, and care that you poured in me throughout my process in Christendom. Thank you for your welcomed input for the title of this book.

To my writing mentor, Prophetess Monika McKay-Polly, of Firestarter Ministries, (also an author) thank you for your prayers and the time you took in pushing me to the different stages in my process in birthing and finishing this assignment. The time you made for me and being a good example in showing your labor of love as an author is well noted and has helped me to stay focused.

Thank you, Tenita Johnson, editor of *So It Is Written* for doing an excellent work with editing my manuscript, for your patience, and your eye for detail with all the preparation that went into it.

Thank you so much, Ms. Shelia Bell, author, editor and formatter at Shelia Writes Books. Your work and input is phenomenal. Thank you for your support and insight in bringing it all together.

Thank you to all who have prayed me through. I love and appreciate you. I can never thank you enough for your passionate prayers and listening to the Spirit of God with an open heart. It has been a wonderful process because of all of you.

Hazel O. Kersellius

"In everything give thanks:
For this is the will of God
in Christ Jesus concerning you."

1 Thessalonians 5.18 KJV

SALVATION

Salvation: "*1*.the act of saving or protecting from harm, risk, loss, destruction, etc. *2*. the state of being saved or protected from harm, risk, etc. *3*. a source, cause, or means of being saved or protected from harm, risk, etc. *4*. Theology. Deliverance from the power and penalty of sin, redemption."

Christ came to save the world for those who believe by faith, to give life more abundantly, and to have a relationship with his people. God has given each of us a purpose. He wants us to know Him standing strong in faith.

We are made in the image and likeness of God. Our identity is found in Christ Jesus. We are saved by no other name. "There is salvation in no one else! God has given no other name under heaven by which we must be saved" (Acts 4:12 NLT).

Many of us invest in insurance for such things as our life, cars, and/or businesses. Consider something that is even more precious—your soul. I experienced salvation by trusting, receiving, and believing by faith of the finished work of the cross. Once you receive salvation "there is therefore now no condemnation to them which are in Christ Jesus..." (Romans 8:1 KJV).

God's grace covers us when we fall short. Rest in the finished work of the cross. Embrace your process. Hold on to the promises of God and your salvation. Repent as needed. God is a loving and forgiving God and He desires a relationship with you.

A Price Was Paid

How Christ paid the price for you and me,
He bore our sins,
The ones we lived in,
Paid in full at Calvary.

What we should have felt
With every lash of the belt,
The spit, the grit, every kick,
The stones that hit his bones—
He felt all alone.

No one lived without sin
To carry what He did undeserved.
The only perfect Sacrificial Lamb,
Sent by The Great I Am.

Who can stand by His side
And not deny Him three times?
To not do what Peter did—
Oh my, heaven forbid!
He was forgiven, yes my friend,
He repented in the end.

Judas was not spared,
For the devil does not care.
Betrayed for the exchange
Of change with a kiss,
He sent himself to an abyss.

Do you understand what the King has done?
To pay for one single sin, we would run.
He cried with tears as unto blood
To our God whom promised
Never to send another flood.

Spent forty days and nights under a fast—
In the wilderness,
Tempted and prodded to fail His task,
To an enemy that will not last.

With the Father, He failed not,
For to pay our price was His lot.
Let us not forget what He's done,
This is God's only begotten Son.
He stretched our faith, miracle by miracle,
Healed the sick with a love that's lyrical.
Taught us all what the Father said—
It's there in the Word, written in red.

A Psalm in my heart, I sing
That you would spread His Word
And this one last thing.
The love He has for you and me
Was felt in spirit before He hung on that tree.
Blaze this world with a fervent love,
As the One that was sent from God up above.

He left His Holy Spirit
As it descended like a dove—
Father, Son, all three in one.
Pray it's your soul He takes,
When it's all said and done.

Work out your own salvation—
God will give you the rhema you need
From Genesis to Revelation.

God's Love for Mankind

Oh, blessed Savior
The one who changed my behavior
From bad and mad to glad,
An everlasting joy.
Tranquility, peace, and serenity.
Once caught in an entangled web
Taking heed to the lessons
Mom and Dad have said,
Getting knowledge and wisdom
And in all my getting,
Understanding I wed.
A relationship with the one who bled
And paid for all my transgressions
Past, present and future,
With love from the Father
He bore our sins with torture.
So that we may live and rein with Him forever.
He died for mankind not going in blind
Conquered sin so we can now win.
He's given us the opportunity
To let Him in Our hearts
And to renew our minds.
That is how much He loves mankind.
Won't you confess Christ is Lord?
Let your heart, mind and confession
Be on one accord.
He loves you that much,
Develop a relationship with Him.
Walk out your faith and He will be pleased,
I can only imagine Him smiling
As His love for you makes you
Look up and inward-saying "...*cheeeeese!*"

Hearken Unto Me, My Sweet

I need you to wait on Me.
Wait, see, taste—
Smell the goodness of the Lord,
My fruit is sweet.

I AM that I AM complete.
Sing it loud to those you meet.

I am good,
You can trust me.
Lean in on me,
Nothing grim found in me.

Hearken unto Me, my sweet creation,
Your soul will be elated.
Your spirit-man will grow—
I am your Father, don't you know?

I make the world glow,
I am slow to anger.
Draw near when you cry,
I will always be by your side.
Keep me near your heart—
I will never depart.
My Spirit will cleave to all your needs.

Just breathe and rest in Me,
Come, taste and see
My agenda is free—
My love, my child, hearken unto Me.
I set the captives *free!*

Identified

He knows my likes and dislikes,
He knows what I'm attracted to and what repulses me.
He has a will for me, don't you see?
God knows your fruit and so does he,
They've both made plans for your destiny.

Who is the other I am speaking of?
He makes counterfeits of God's goodness and love,
Including using the symbol of the upside down dove.
Once an archangel that fell from heaven and grace
Because iniquity and pride was found in him,
He was cast out.
He fell on his face.

Once called Lucifer and the morning star.
This prince of the air sells you lies,
Keeping you from living in the fullness of who you are.
Count your blessings that
You are justified by the Lord's death,
And His resurrection—how nice.
God is all you need, and the Holy Spirit will suffice.

The one on the throne interceding for you
Is God the Son, named Jesus Christ.
Individually and as one,
Filling all your voids.
Make sure Satan does not get a foothold,
Dangling and enticing you to the world's ways like toys.

He is not to be played with,
He's after your soul.
Prostrate yourself before the Lord,
Come boldly before His throne,
You are identified by God in Christ.

You have access to
And are filled with the Holy Spirit.
Come to know your authority,
You're a warrior.
Use it!

Take the enemy by force
And with violent prayer.
He is no joke—slay him and his army,
Together at once with the Word,
Not just layer by layer.

There will be a time to rest, but the battle is on.
"Greater is he that is in you than he that is in the world."
Let that be your song.
Rise up and blow the shofar 'til the break of dawn.
Use your keen discernment, for the
Enemy's high volume of deception is on.

Listen for the Holy Spirit's cue,
His strategy, and wait on His timing,
For going in with a small number
To face his legion lays the Lord's victory.
You can in your spirit-man start smiling.

This battle is done.
Don't you know?
Christ already conquered death.
He's God's shining Son.
We already won,
When God accepted the perfect sacrifice
And gave glory to His Son.
God sees you through His blood.
Its power goes deeper than what's generally understood.

When you eat of that bread and drink of that cup,
Taste of that wine—
Remember the work is finished,
The Holy sacrament is truly divine.
He paid the price for you,
Not like how He was betrayed
For mere shekels, like minuscule dimes.

He laid down His life and picked it back up
So that one day, He may reign with you
And sup from His everlasting cup.
Praising God's name,
Your Majesty's train
Fills the temple.
We will freely worship Him into eternity,
It's just that simple.

Formed in His image and likeness,
We are identified by God Almighty,
And by no other name,
Are we reconciled back to God.
That's why Christ came.

By accepting in our heart
And confessing Christ's sacrifice.
The one who immaculately was conceived
Through Mary, His mother.
Now my child, go tell your sisters and brothers.
Identified by the Holy Trinity and demons, too.
Feed your spirit with the Word of God.
Prayer, praise and worship, that's true,
For the Spirit of God is jealous for you!

It's a Gift

I used to think life was a game,
Constantly hiding from my shame.
Then I'd exploit the sin I was in,
Since it started from the Garden of Eden.

But then I came to realize my soul
Was in the threshold of a fiery demise.
I needed to repent
For all that wicked time spent
Against the will of God.

It wasn't enough to know Him,
I had to let His only begotten Son in
My heart with my chin held high,
For I know His return is nigh.
I want to be caught up in the sky,
In front of the Father so I won't be denied.

For those caught up in pride—
For the backslider,
Those up to their chin in sin,
I beg you—
Let Christ in.

Don't be blind.
This is a war for souls
And you can win
When you just let Him in.

Don't find yourself in a ditch
Or fellowshipping with a witch.
God knows and sees it all,
From the great to the very small.
Make a switch

Before His judgment falls,
And you find yourself in the pit of the weaker power.
He is sufficient to bring you out.

Can you feel your soul cry out?
Repent and confess with your mouth, "Christ is Lord."
It's a gift.
When you accept, you've already won.
Let go of the past - what's done is done.
Begin to praise Him,
Don't run.

He will work it out in your favor,
So much goodness to savor.
Do it now while there is time,
His Love and Grace is truly sublime.

Meditate on His Word day and night
So your spirit will be inclined to do what's right.
God is awesome,
He's dyno-mite!
Keep your prayer life very bright.

For the saints will judge the earth, you see,
Not to condemn, but to set order.
Start seeing beyond the borders.
Greater are you in Him,
Than you reveling in all that sin.

The Final Say

Death in the night
Comes in quick flight
While you rest your heart.
It's like a violent knock at the door—
And an urgent call awaits to meet
Your maker once more.

To sit at the seat of judgment
And answer and make an account for
All the years He's blessed you out loud
For the world to see.
As you answer, there's no one to see,
Except Elohim, The One.

But the question will be:
Have you accepted Him?
Have you let the Lord in your heart?
And attack your iniquity?
And fill your heart with love, peace, and tranquility?

Passing all tests to show your purified love?
'Tis my hope that your relationship
Was unto a beautiful friendship, too.
And not for Him to say—
"Depart from me, I never knew you."

Either way, He's made himself known,
For you to make your choice with a 'Yes' or a 'No'.
The final evaluation is God's, you see.
You just don't want to hear,
"Depart from me ..."

The final say comes from your sum of
Choices you make in life every day.

No one goes to the Father, except through the Son.
Yes, He's the only One.

Many miss the mark
By believing in philosophies
That keep you in the dark.
Question who or what's in your heart.
Search and work out your own soul salvation.
Count it as your personal revelation.
For tomorrow is not promised to anyone,
But forever can start today,
If you'll allow Christ to lead the way.

The Light in the Dark

The sun goes down, the town gets dark,
But my heart has a lighted spark
That transcends earthly time as
My soul rejoices of things in heavenly places.
What joy I feel
At times, I ask, "Is this real?"

It must be true as my faith stands strong
Against the wiles of the enemy—
For he has failed and his legion dumb, fallen,
In the dark without a spark, full of lies,
Fear and deception.

In the end will be a hellish reception,
But oh no, not for I,
For my heart has loved
The One who sits on high.

At His right hand,
Not founded on sinking sand.
Oh how grand His love, for you and me.
He fully paid the cost–hung on a tree.

He gave his life for you and me,
Don't stop now, sing it proud.
It is His will and Spirit that draws us in crowds.

Praise Him LOUD and in your humbled hearts.
He loved you readily from the start.
His work is done, the masterpiece complete.
His work does not need a repeat.
Holy Spirit, do not grieve,
Father, Son, You are three in one.
My heart—enraptured for what you've done.

From sunset to sundown, you're with me—
My happy pill.
I taste, I see, I touch, I smell, I hear.

Your Word you speak—my prayers entreat.
Your visions to me so clear –
No word spared,
Your word declared.

Apostle, prophet, evangelist, pastor,
Teacher, a five-fold ministry,
I found it here.
St. Albans Gospel Assembly,
I always look forward to seeing you there!

Who Am I?

Dear Lord,
I am yours. But who am I?
In my eyes,
Which see in a limited view
Seems to me—
That I am shy, have pride, and fell many times.

Then I discovered you—
My Creator.
Grander than the ocean's shore,
Wider than the deep blue sky.
Higher than the thrill of a mountain's heights.

You reach deeper than the valley's core,
Lower than the greatest sea floor,
Wiser than man's best philosophy.
Of all you created, why did you create me?
What is my purpose in thee?
Please tell me, who am I?

You, my child, are mine, paid with a price.
Once you've accepted Him I can begin...
The real masterpiece.
The Holy Spirit will guide you.

My Son will bind you
From your spirit man's effect from sin
When you confess and let Him in your heart.

I, your Father, will complete the love I made
And placed in you my child,
So let's start.
You are my precious likeness in my image,
Strong and knitted the way I wanted.

Precious to me, oh, how sweet.
You don't have to be perfectly neat,
For you are made perfect in me.
I called you to be holy, for I am Holy.
Hold me dear to your heart,
That is where my work starts.
I love you dearly. Do you hear me?
Do not allow the enemy to sing my truth contrary—
For he is a lie ready to cause confusion,
When I make plain his delusions.

I love you dearly.
Do you hear me?
Love me back with all your soul and might,
Everything will be alright.
Through the sun and storm
Oh, what fruit you'll bear.
Always know you're in my care.
But, your love, I will not split nor share.
Please do not test me
I will always give you the best of me.

Oh, how I love thee,
My precious child.
Born again, meek and mild.
You are my precious child.
And I will always love you dearly.
You just don't know,
How I love you so!

PRAISE & WORSHIP

Praise: "The act of expressing approval or admiration; commendation, laudation. 2. The offering of grateful homage in words or song, as an act of worship."

Worship: "Reverent honor and homage paid to God or a sacred personage, or to any object regarded as sacred. 2. Formal or ceremonious rendering of such honor and homage."

Worship is an expression to God with a reverent fear. In Christianity, we reverence God with a reverent fear, not fear as in being afraid, but being in awe of who God is.

It is good to praise and worship God. Praise and worship release blessings, revelation, and instructions. Praising and worshipping God did not always come natural for me. At first I tried imitating others. Soon my heart posture in worship came from a sincere and honest place to tell God how good He has been to me. My worship may not look like yours. I may lift God up with praise. I may worship in my obedience, in song, dance, raised hands, reading His Word or meditating on His goodness. However you choose to praise and worship, let it be in spirit, in truth and from a sincere place.

God honors praise and worship. He is attracted to our faith, praise and worship. In everything it is good to give thanks (1 Thessalonians 5:18, KJV).

Expressions
for the Lover of My Soul

Expressed words of gratitude
With the utmost, respectful, humble attitude.
You've created me before I was conceived in spirit.
So my love for you grows,
and I want the world to hear it.

How you loved me first
Before my mother birthed—
Me into this world.
Now amongst the living,
My expression of gratitude keeps on giving.
Like a flowing river,
I never could out give the ultimate giver.
You have created me in your likeness and image,
An expression that is fearfully and wonderfully made.

I look up to see your rainbow of promise,
A cascade of rich colors,
A covenant made
That you will not flood the earth again.
Although, my heart is drowning daily,
Engulfed in your ever present
Love, peace, joy, mercy and grace.
A growing relationship with you Lord,
Ever seeking your face.

You are the Lover of my soul.
It is your desire that I live and not die.
You promised to wipe away every tear I've cried.
Only you can make me whole,
In the mirror, I see a reflection of me in you
A true expression for the Lover of my soul.

For Your Glory

I want to thank you. Lord for loving me.
Your love, mercy and grace protected me.
Your strength in me set me free.
I love you, Lord for loving me.
I got to tell you right now,
Your truth is sweet.

Your love set the captive free.
I know, I know, I know that included me!
Take me higher, take me now.
Take me higher, my heart bows.
No more idols. No golden cows.
I want to see your promise land sooner… now.
I love you Lord. I love you – WOW.

Your creations, the seeds you've sown,
Your Heavenly and earthly realm is blown
In great power, so you're known.
All you give, I give it back to you—
Blessing your name, for you are true.

I love you, Lord.
Yes, indeed.
Thank you, Lord for planting seeds.
May I grow for your glory
Honor, might and power.

To live holy through the last hour,
Or shall we say forever and ever.
To live right—
To be seen just in your sight,
You guide my paths,
Making even my enemies do what's right.
That's your power, that's your might.

It is your will that none should die,
Push back Satan and all his lies.
He will flee to no surprise.

Live by faith in God with the Lord on your side.
For in this, there is everything,
For this world owes you nothing.
In this, there is something,
I will tell you again—
This world owes you nothing.

For your glory, I live for you only.
Killing my flesh daily, making my temple holy.
I live for His Glory.
He is perfect to the 'T'.
Trust in Him, not in me—
I am bowing at His feet!

Homage to the Holy Spirit

Holy Spirit,

You have been there since the beginning of time,
With God the Father and God the Son,
Each fully God—together you're one.
Your work is magnificent,
You are the Spirit that hovered the earth—
Parted the seas, giving it birth.
You are the breath of life that entered man.
You are the Great I AM.

When the first man ate what seemed to be a prize,
It truly was death to our soul's demise.
Our spirit man died to thee,
When beguiled by the enemy in Genesis Chapter 3.
But even then God, you made a way,
When your Holy Spirit embodied in Christ
'Til He died on Crucifixion Day.

Before Christ ascended and
Immediate visitations ended,
He breathed on them the Holy Ghost
So all who believed in Him
Would be comforted from coast to coast.

You are the Comforter and so much more.
There's much to learn of you and explore.
You convict our souls
When we commit unjustly woes.
You are a person that can grieve
Though you, we cannot see.

When we can't pray, but just moan,
You intercede,
When all we can do is just *breathe.*

"Who are you?" some would say
You are the power of God,
Still alive and active 'til this very day.
You love, speak, give revelation, have a will,
Yet omnipotent, omniscient, omnipresent still.
You are the resurrection power
That raised the dead and Christ in that holy hour.
You are the Spirit that moves
When we speak in tongues.
You give creation to many reverent songs.

Oh, you baptize with your Holy fire.
In you, our worship grows higher and higher.
Holy Ghost, you inspired the scribes to write.
Your words in the Word guide man to live right.
With every breath and day by day,
You make living very bright in an exciting way—
What can we say?

This Christ said before I close.
There is one last thing you must know—
Do not blaspheme Him or His name.
For in this, there's no forgiveness
And your soul's fate will not be the same.
In this life or the next,
Do not put God to that test.
He loves you more than I can see,
I'm sure you can all agree.
Holy Spirit, you give such love,
You're represented as a dove.

We love all of who you are,
All of what you do,
This is true.
And all what you say.
So we celebrate you too
On this Easter Sunday.

In the Still of the Night

In the still of the night
The Lord bids me to come.
He covers me with His peace
To be still and know He's the One.

In the still of the night,
Know He is God.
He doesn't need my help,
Though my permission, He does—
To submit my will to His because
He gave me a choice concerning my life.

For to love Him on purpose is what He loves,
Without grief nor strife.
To do His will is to prove my love.
And in doing so, I set Him above all else.

I set Him above mankind,
Every need, desire, and supply
For God, you are my provider.
In you, you take me higher and higher
From the intricacies of my breath,
To the growth of my hair,
The blink of my eyes,
To every tear I've cried.

My heart beats for you,
My heart waits for you
To give me the Zoë in my mouth.
From there, my worship springs out.
Oh, how I'll sing your praise
For the rest of my days.
I'll give you praise!

I'm honored in you,
I glory in your truth.
All this I do, just to give it back to you.

God, I bless you.
I honor you!
Thank you for seeing all of me,
Even parts no one else sees.
Yet, you still choose to love me
For all you've called me to be,
And you love me so freely.

I ask that you bless me in a special way
Where no one else can say,
It was them who made my day.
For no one to steal your glory,
I worship you and you only.

Keep me in your graces,
As your love takes me into great levels
And heavenly places.
This I ask as I grow in you,
As my faith pleases you,
As I lay my life down for you,
For I want to see you!
The one who loved me first,
In spirit and in truth, I bless you,
For you only, I thirst.

My Maestro

How great is thy love and tender mercies?
Captivating love!
A magnet to my soul.
By your shed blood, I'm made whole.
How amazing,
You did that for me,
Hung on that rugged cross at Calvary.
You opened my blind eyes, Lord,
Making me to see
How you loved me in spite of me.
I will forever praise your name,
Your love is a mystery
Though it surpasses all understanding.
Every breath I take comes from you,
A life you've given me.
I reflect on your Word having tea,
Listening to Handel's Concerti Grossi—a symphony!
You're a masterpiece that fills the air I breathe.
Teach me to see others the way you see me.
I'm an instrument, my Maestro.
Conduct me at your will.
I will strike the chord that sings –
Lord! Lord! Lord!
You rise in my heart in the morning skies
And set in my thoughts, making me wise
Beyond the scope, my sweet surprise!
In me, you are alive.
Known to man, yes this is true.
But so many have yet to *really* know you.

Diligently seek Him, my song plays,
And my Maestro will be found of you, too.
Conduct Maestro.
Do your will.
Many, many souls to begotten still.
I'll bow when I reach the heavens, and even now.
This is my Maestro.
Please allow—
Him to conduct your life.
You will see He is worth the prize.
Standing ovations,
Many, many times.
Let my Maestro take you by surprise.
Allow Him to entreat, His music is sweet,
Encore! Encore!
I bow because
He is the Maestro Master of my soul,
And I LOVE HIM!

The Breath of God

God, your breath is an essence of your Spirit.
Holy, Holy, Holy, we can feel it.
It heals and gives direction,
Fills my lungs with peace, love, and affection,
In the midst of it, you reveal revelation.

Your breath gives us life.
From Adam to the latest generation of mankind—
You are the Great I AM.
I am to you what you'll have me to be.
I am your servant–a fruit-bearing fig tree.

God, you're second to none.
In you— I won with your Son.
Your breath birthed the Great Comforter to us
To lead me, guide me, stand right beside me.
Your breath is one essence of who you are,
Filling my presence like a morning star.

There's such a peace from you
When you release your breath.
I will take of you and give back to you,
Even until death.

Lord, I bid you to occupy this place
As you fill yourself in the realm of
Heaven, earth, and space.

Nothing is out of place,
You're everywhere at once.
For if I can just breathe in a trace of you,
Oh, what miraculous works you will do.

Hence, I am reminded that your Holy Spirit
Healed me completely, with just a breath from you.
All I need is a touch from you,
And I'm made whole—
Body, mind, and soul.

Lord, I thank you and breathe in your effervescence.
I welcome you once more—your Holy presence.
Let not pride nor unforgiveness cause us to miss it.
I am here for only an instant.

Until I see you face to face,
In your glorious heavenly place.
I inhale and exhale that which
You've caused me to rest in—
Your mercy and grace.

What I Desire of You

I give you wealth, I give you health,
I, not the world, am the Undergirding Belt.
Do not fear while the world depletes.
Rest assured, I'm the one who fulfills the needs.
Give your offering of praise,
The sacrifice of giving me worship,
For worship was the reason I made you.
Try my Spirit by the spirit.
For that's how I commune with you.
Do you receive it?
There is nothing I will hold from you.
For the treasures I placed in you
I call forth to see what you will do.
Be true to the love I give you.
For all I have, and all I give,
With all I know and
All I AM and All I show—
Your worship
Is what I desire of you. Now you know.
This day, I am with you, do not be dismayed,
Come boldly before me and lift your praise.
For that's what you'll do for the rest of your days.
I want your worship and your praise.

LOVE

Love: "*1*. A profoundly tender, passionate affection for another person.... *12*. The benevolent affection of God for his creatures, or the reverent affection due from them to God."

The Word of God tells us what it is to love. "Love is patient and kind. Love is not jealous or boastful or proud or rude. It does not demand its own way. It is not irritable, and it keeps no record of being wronged. It does not rejoice about injustice but rejoices whenever the truth wins out. Love never gives up, never loses faith, is always hopeful and endures through every circumstance" (1 Corinthians 13:4-7 NLT).

God tells us to love. There are four types of love: eros, storge, philia, and agape. Eros is the romantic or sensual love. Storge is the love one has for family. Philia is expressed love for others. Agape is God's unconditional love for mankind. In this chapter *love* deals with having a fondness for a place, friendship, understanding God's love, ideas of love, feelings of love, and expressing what it feels like to be loved.

A Taste of Home

I just may turn into a Georgia Peach,
With all that sunshine and starry sky,
Lemon Meringue and Apple Pie.

Let me shut my mouth—
Before I get a taste
Of that good ol' South.

Oh, how I miss it so,
Lots of land spread out low
Makes me really want to know.

It has a charm of its own,
A place I can always call home.

Like good ol' Clarkesville, Tennessee—
A place I hold very dear to me.

Best Friends

Best friends can change
Or may remain the same for years to come.
Some you outgrow,
Some are just for show.

But when it's mutual,
The sky is the limit.
Rising to an endless sky—
On a wonderful balloon ride.

Then that friend that was best
May be second guessed,
And the framework may be redefined.

Leaving an open space to be filled
By someone true
Who has an open heart
And compassion to forgive you—
To uphold one another 'til the end of time.

Facets of God's Love

How would I describe the love of God?
His love wraps around the bride and groom,
Overflows to the child in her womb.
It flourishes around the world to see.
He loves so willing and unselfishly.

He loves deep beyond the levels
Of what the eye can see.
He loves like a whirlwind parting the seas,
Crossing His people from the front line of the enemy.

He plants life and death with a single breath.
With a thought
He calls the stars to line up—
Just where they are.
Not one orbit is too narrow or too far.

He shifts creation with a touch of His love—
Causing mankind to return to His first love.
His only Son whom He gave,
To proxy against the dark knave.
God's love caused Him to remove Christ from the cave,
So we can witness His bliss.
It's time to move from our self-reliant thinking,
And take the risk.

To lean on the Holy Spirit for all of our needs,
My heart, soul, mind, and spirit now see.
To love, to give my life as I know it
And allow Him to take the lead,
Then show it.

Facets of Love

Love grows and flutters and blows,
awaiting the change currents as it lays low.
Love grows, skipping and brushing along top soil,
Awaiting the weight of rain to merge the seed in earth.
Love breathes the breath of life and is
the Creator whom creates infinity, the life of other
creations.
Love pulls you from the insides—
From the center.
Love flutters like an excitable butterfly and is as
abundant as a peppery Pekingese.
As ravishing as a majestic stallion and as bold as a lion.
As blind as a bat, it prances from within you like a wild
cat on an attack.
It finds the most intriguing ball of yarn fascinating.
It taps the most inanimate and gives it life.
Love camouflages to match the comfort zone
to give you security that it is there in the right measure.
Love doesn't starve.
Love breathes joy, peace and goodwill.
Love protects all sides.
Love lets go.
Love lets God.
All in all, love is God and
God is beyond what my heart can fully understand.

I Want Pure Love

I want pure love made for me,
That loves you more than I can see.
To pour my love like liquid silk,
Made of fine gold, sapphire, ruby, and pearls.
Make our sky as bright as Skittle rainbows.
The sign of promise.
Never send another flood of despair of lost love.

Saturate my heart with passion, peace, and joy.
Rain upon me healing for my pain,
Deliver me once again
Until I'm made whole—
Until pure love remains.

Make our laughter break cedar wood,
And take this world by storm.
We'll praise your name 'til the break of dawn.

As a unit, you're the head.
We'll birth sons and daughters of God—
Bringing forth prophets, pastors,
Teachers, evangelists,
And apostles, too.
One body, yet all parts of you—
Your Spirit.

Can you hear it,
The sound of praise?
Our family will forever exalt your name.
May it be a sweet sound in your ear,
With fear in reverence to you,
For our worship must be true,
And in spirit, too.

God, my Lord, we love you.
Our life in you—
A treasure.
A living sacrifice, nothing else can satisfy
Or be better, but our walk in faith in you.

Loving your only Son,
Believing and confessing what He's done.
The walk is long and has just begun.
But as long as we are faithful—
For the battle is won.

Season Romance

Beautiful gardens bloom in spring.
Birds fly with songs to sing.
Flowers sweet with dripping dew
From far away trees,
Shading the essence that nature is calling.

Hearts are yawning for the awakening
Of summer romance.

Pound for pound,
Hearts are on an enchanting race.
There's no finish—
Just a change of course.

Fluffy white bunnies, prancing
In a wide open field of green prairies—

Lightly brushing sun on stems that
Are dandy and secure like lions.

Wherefore art thy love in bloom
In wanting in bated breath?
Behold in the midst of season romance.

The Questionable Date

Can you talk to me with a thrill of excitement,
With love and perhaps with bated breath
That tells me
That I'm desired much by you?

If so, that makes two—
Of us.
Next is trust.
Can I share my dreams?
The ones that send emotions to extremes?
In making them happen?
How open can I be?
Will you see me for me?

Shall we discuss this,
Perhaps over a cup of tea,
Beneath an old oak tree?
Inspire me.
Why should I be shy?
No need for pride.
I having nothing to hide—
Tell me, what is a lovely man like you doing by my side?

Do you have a soul God can trust?
Do you desire true love, or
Do you confuse it for lust?

When it comes to the issues of life,
Do you trust in Christ, or
Do you roll the dice,
Then pay a worldly price?

I've cried many tears—
Been celibate for years.
Don't think you can just pick me up
In a bar like *Cheers*
God knows what I need—
A man who can praise the Lord,
Using the best of musical chords,
Not someone sold out for the world.

Do you cry out to Him?
Have you repented of past sins?
When you get God's business straight—
I'll be ready to take the bait.

Even then, I'll seek counsel for my
Love is not for sale.
It must be sealed in holy matrimony
Your love for me—
And I for you only.
I'd love a family that lives holy.
Now tell me,
What's your story—
Mr. Lonely?

HOPE

Hope: "1. The feeling that what is wanted can be had or that events will turn out for the best. 2. To look forward to with desire and reasonable confidence....3. To believe or desire or trust."

As Christians, when we have hope, we put our trust in God, for in Him do we move, live, and have our being. God says if we trust Him, He will not fail us. We can trust Him because God is reliable. He is perfect. God says, "I am the way, the truth and the life: no man cometh to the Father, but by me" (John 14:6 KJV). "...There is no evil in Him" (Psalm 92:15 NLT).

I have hope in God. There are times when no one will have the right answer and wisdom you need to remedy your problem, but God will always lead you to someone that can help. Be open to how God is leading and directing you.

I put my trust in God and go to God first. My hope is in God alone. Man will fail you, but God will never fail you. He is the King of kings and our Hope in Glory.

Can the Eye See Itself?

Can the eye see itself?
No.
Only if you look in the mirror.
Who shall that mirror be, you or me,
Or the one true living God?
For if I see my eyes in that mirror
That speaks back to me,
I run the risk of pure vanity.
If I let you tell me what you see,
Your spirit may impart
An inaccurate report of me.
One that's not of necessity,
Nor the just in full balance
You see in me.

But, *ahh.*
The God who made the birds in the trees
And the fish of the sea,
The One who owns all of the cattle on a thousand hills.
The God who knows
The plans for you and me
Can see all things, just and pure,
Not in folklore.

I dare not ask the universe,
For He created it.
I'd rather go to my source.
For He relayed His Word for me to see,
His truth can now reside within me.

As my spirit
Is convicted by the Holy Spirit,
I see when I read His truth—
I can stand.

I am made right
In His sight,
From the very moment I receive Christ.

I am victorious.
A mighty woman of valor.
I pick up my cross
And march on through this spiritual battle.

Let no man in any land in anywise,
Counsel thee in unrighteousness.
Where do you stand?
For His Kingdom is at hand.

Why veer off to say,
 "...the universe gave the blessing,"
When God created both?
It has always been God who gives it—
Love, knowledge, wisdom, understanding,
Provision in abundance,
Success and ambition
For His glorification.
No needed explanation.
Don't make up a story,
Simply give God His glory.

Mighty in battle, my Lord has won.
He has won the battle for my soul,
This soul you see through the windows of my eyes.

He feeds my spirit.
Yes, you can feel it when He touches it.
No, you can't see it, but He ministers to it.
Only He has access to us that way
As He fills me, heals me and stands right beside me.

Now and when I pray,
All I have come to know as I grow in Christ,
Is to stay in His Word,
Pray and obey.
For to obey is greater than sacrifice,
And will more than suffice.

Be ye transformed by the renewing of your mind.
Read His Word and your reflection you will find.
Soon those eyes you see,
Is a reflection that God is pleased with me.

Coming Into Truth

Letting go of false beliefs
And coming to the truth that chiefs
All of what you thought you knew,
And learn of God, who always knew.

Take part in His sovereignty,
Which opposes His enemies' words of blasphemy.
Study His word, which is tried and true.
Take up His delicious fruit.
His word is marrow to your bones,
Filled with promises that you'll never be alone.

How would I know?
I've tasted of His fruit for myself,
And stopped putting hearsay on the shelf.
I've given my heart to the King
And made a point to learn of the beginning--
Through His word, washed by His blood,
Basking in His everlasting love,
I gain insight to my elevation
While I experience His divine revelation.

When you come to the truth,
What will you do?
Follow acts of religion,
Which is indignation to His grace?
His gift of salvation does have a place.

Don't take the credit for it,
Our deeds would never pay the debt of it.
To what we truly owe.
It is the love He has for us,
For our sins, He died for us
And has let our obligation go.

Don't take the fall, mixing truth with lies,
Which scatter His sheep to His wailing outcry.
Accountability will be made when a head
Has twisted what God has said.
It only takes a little bad leaven to spoil bread
When what's said is not what He meant.

Seek His truth and all of it,
People do die from lack of it.
Pray against any counterfeit.
When you come to the heart of it.
You will know to seek Him,
Do so with all your heart, might and strength,
And know it was emphatically worth it.

Day by Day…

When your heart bows low
And there's no point where you would not go,
Call my name, but not in vain.
I will come riding down from the sky.
I am nigh to your point of hopelessness.
I will bless you to bliss
In ways unknown to your ways.

Especially when you pray.
Pray to me, day by day,
Moment by moment,
Minute by minute—
Unceasingly.

'Til your soul is enraptured in spirit.
With all your soul—
Come bold to my throne.

And I will honor my will to you,
As your faithfulness remains true.
Oh, how I love you—
I really and truly love you.

I AM the one
Who sent my only begotten Son
To die for you—
This is my immeasurable love
From me to you.

Dream Supreme

My days are filled with business
Until I rest my head in the still of the night,
Drifting to a place of wonder—
A place of splendor.
Moving from left to right.

Hoping not one nightmare will enter.
Hoping for a beautiful dream supreme
Of adventure, that no enemy will enter.

Will my guards stand near?
As my angels are dear, pushing aside all fear.

'Tis clear.
That the Lord has connected me to all that's right—
And has warned me of things to be rebuked in this
life.

To dream a dream, there's much to be said.
God has breathed into me, life,
I'm far from dead.
Nothing but sugarplums dancing in my head.

'Til morning shines again—
And again His love is mine.
As I go about my business of my newly blessed day.

Fly!

When it's time to fly,
God will let you fly.
Forget about how,
Or why, with whom,
Or when.

If there is a stumbling stone,
Do not utter, "Again?."
You may stumble upon ten.
That ten will get you to
Fly again and again.

When it's time to fly,
You will fly.
When you join forces
With God's will,
You will soar!

Let Us Adore Him

I give you gifts of joy for every girl and boy—
Woman, man, and child—
Keep your spirit humble, meek, and mild.
Keep me near your heart.
I will destroy the fiery darts
Of the zero one,
In me, you have won.

This Christmas Eve
I bid you to receive
My Spirit of new joy.
The Zoë
Of my revelation.
I'll tear down every worldly abomination.
In me, you are free.
My people, I bid you rest in me.

I will comfort you for every bruise.
I leave it to you to choose,
And leave your cares at the altar.
I AM your Rock of Gibraltar.

Every secret thing, in you and
Of you, is known in my light.
Give it to me
With your lips
And I will flip the script
From dark to light.
I desire you this day in my marvelous light.

I was born for you in a manger
In a time of evident danger.
Though I was small,
I came to make all things new for all.

Continue to bring your gifts of praise and worship,
Believe me, it's here reaching my throne.
You, my sons and daughters, are never alone.

In your spirit lies the kingdom in me.
I'll show up as you rest in me.
At my throne are heavenly hosts,
Dispatching angels for every prayer note.

I will birth in you a new thing.
Let all your heart, mind and soul sing.
I'll wrap your cares with all of me.
Step into this new place and you shall see.

My sons and daughters, just rest in me
And I will do a new thing.
I love it when you sing.
Yes, I will do a new thing.

My Father's Timing

Do you know what it's like to be last in a family
That will not tarry,
To ask when it will be your turn to marry
Or have one of your own?
They wish your circumstances to be cloned,
With your siblings, especially at special gatherings,
As they totally disregard God's special timing.

Your path is not your own
Once you've submitted your will to His.
Having babies is not showbiz.
Marriage is not a chaser after soiled past relationships.
It's a covenant and ministry,
Sanctified between you and the Holy Trinity.

So, please wait.
Let God's timing unfold.
You're not too old,
Your heart will not wax cold.
Come bold before His throne,
Like a passionate praying Hannah.
She put her faith in me,
And I blessed her with a godly seed.

Let the gainsayers talk
About your tick, tock biological clock.
You serve the Inventor of time.
All is well. *All is sublime.*

Remember to whom your members belong,
It's not to mankind's negative song—
Concerned that your clock is abnormally long,
Or that your children may come out all wrong?

Sing to me woman of my likeness.
I'll provide bone of your bone, flesh of your flesh,
I decree that you will not be alone unless—
I call you to a place of singleness.
Even then, I am with thee.
You're considered blessed.
I will surround you with my divine love.
Set me in your life far above man's love.

Though I call you to marry,
Do not idolize a man in marriage.
Don't allow my favor and blessings
On you to be a miscarriage.

I am your Lord,
Praise me single-heartedly.
Let me become your holy family.

My God, My Lord, My Healer

I am at the crossroads of my faith,
Not wanting to waiver, but battling the wait.
Wanting my healing
And claiming my Lord's stripes—
Meditating on these scriptures day and night.

By your stripes, I am healed.
Slain for our iniquity,
How good of a God you are to me.
How sinful of a person I must be.
You took my place.
It should have been me.
I reach for my faith and I look at my disease.
I am at the crossroads—
My belief is on "E".
I haven't read or prayed as much,
Nor have I allowed your truth to truly touch
My heart of hearts.
It's buried somewhere.
I look at my dis-ease and I feel scared.

Then a tear comes to my eyes.
I think about all the reasons that you died.
I take a breath, then firmly decide
To walk in your love,
Read every Word…
You're even interceding for me this very moment.
I place you above all my fears.
At this point, I am drowning in my tears.

How you loved me before this point—
Over two thousand years.
You made the world and toiled for my soul,
Died on the cross and from the grave you rose,

So that I may be whole.
What is it for me to not push aside,
All you fought for and for me to fight the lies—
With your truth?
I got to get this thing.
I'm in need of your healing.
A sister needs Christ to be her wings!

Lord, you fed the hungry twice,
Once on two different occasions
With fish and loaves of bread.
That is what the Word says.
You love me so much.
You left your Holy Spirit
So we are always in touch—
With Him.

My God guides me
And stands right beside me.
I believe it's time to step out on faith
And do what the psalmist, David said—
To be of good courage and wait.
I will wait on your cue and partake of your bread.
I choose this day to receive and
Acknowledge all that you've said
Concerning my health and all of my prosperity.
Line my faith up according to your will and sovereignty.
Eradicate any unbelief found in me.
You are my Healer.
I choose to walk out my faith and make it stellar
And anchor myself as a complete bonafide believer.

The Faithful Soldier

Empty—
Drained—
An open vessel receiving God's love.
Needing to be filled.
Passing tidal waves of emotions,
Keeping rough winds at bay.
The land is dry and rich.

On good ground the dove will stay.
Chasing dreams that seem of old...
Dreams that haven't bloomed, left untold.
Keeping hope refreshed,
For it is God our Lord alone
Who makes all things new.
The journey of faith seems old and new,
And has not long begun.

Fading designs on a blanket of affairs,
This life takes me through.
I hold on for the promise and give God glory
For all honor and glory truly belongs to you.

Coming into purpose...
Coming into the light, it is in God the eternal.
Father, through Christ, I give my life.
For those who give their life over will gain it,
And those who keep it will lose it.
We toil, knowing our destiny comes with a price—

And has been paid
Long ago with the blood of Jesus Christ.
Anchor firm I say.
Pray back His word.

Keep your faith
In the one true living God.
For the world's ways are
Like tides in the ocean—
And the winds of the sea,
Not knowing when or which way the
Fallen branch will pass or how long it will settle.

Christ is my Rock.
So I toil with purpose.
I press forward.
Like a good and faithful soldier—
Troop's attention!
About face!
Onward march!
I say keep the good faith,
And stand.

The Process

Oh Lord, when the stings of life hit you
With great turbulence,
With great strife,
How do I prevent my soul
From recoiling to that dark place
Where fear and anger and shame remains?
Guilt holding me up, like stilts having a posture to fall.
Lord, please take me far from this place.
Where love's fruit is bare and the bitterness
Has usurped all sweetness,
And its succulence has turned violently dry
In a desolate place.
I pray you pull me from this pit of darkness,
That my life will be a testimony as you hold my cares
With a union of holy matrimony.
Teach me your ways,
Fill my days with sunshine,
Replenish my heart's wellspring with joy.
May my nights be protected,
As guards of the night,
Like watchmen guarding treasure
As you would with my soul.
Behold, my Maker, let your glory shine like the dawn
And your Spirit settle upon me as unto dusk,
In you I put my trust.
Help me to believe with all my heart
In areas that are blocked from you.
Mold me and make me who you've called me to be.
Help me to see and know you internally, for all eternity,
With a life transformed,
Make me born again,
Changed from living a life of sin.
Please begin your masterpiece in me.
I thank you now, for the process.

Victory

Oh, why? Oh, why?
Some days feel like rain.
A feeling of pain
Inside, my heart thunders again.

When clouds subside,
Hoping the winds won't drift,
Making any unwelcomed shift.
To rise above the height of plight
In a swift and quick
One-two fight.

In the end, to know and feel that
Life has served its battles—
Very real.
Just to feel and know
the taste of *victory!*

DELIVERANCE

Deliverance: "*1*. An act or instance of delivering *2*. Salvation *3*. Liberation *4*. A thought or judgment expressed, a formal or authoritative pronouncement."

When God delivers us it is an act of setting us free from bondage, demonic spirits, enemies, circumstances or a state of mind, body, or identity that keeps us from walking contrary to living life abundantly and according to His will.

There is no one way for a person to be delivered. Some may be delivered through song, worship, prayer, fasting, and can be right at home. Some strongholds are generational. Others are self-inflicted or are a result of decisions made and now it has the person in bondage.

Regardless of how the stronghold came to be, God can deliver and set you free. Be open to the move of God. Be sure to give Him all the glory. Matthew 17:21 KJV: "Howbeit this kind goeth not out but by prayer and fasting."

Do Not Lie to Me

Do not lie to me
While I reside in you,
My spirit of truth.
Do not grieve me with lies, bribes, or any excuse.
Do not compromise for the sake of an "innocent" sin.
You made a deal with me when you let me in.

Do not renege to please man.
It defeats the principle.
Make the truth monumental—
Because it is.

The dark principalities of this earth were found on a lie
When I, he denied.
With vain imaginations, as if I should serve him.
This I quickly casted down
Deception is embodied as a snake—
Belly hugging the ground.
Do not make what's low your lord,
I made you in my likeness to be on one accord.

I need to trust you,
even when no one is around
Make your integrity profound.
I will confound the deceiver to make you a believer.

There in the midst I stand, 'til the ends of the earth,
As far as the heavens—
I want my Spirit in thee to leaven.

So, please do not lie to me
While you serve me, do it with probity.
Be good, faithful, and true
As you represent me with glee,
Producing good fruit on your tree.

Intercessor for the Unbeliever

Don't just walk away and not pray for me,
I too, need the seed God placed in thee.
Despite my unbelief,
My reprobate mind may end in grief.
If you know the power
that prayer can have on me,
Please go into your secret closet
and pray for me.
I struggle with the world,
my spirit in God is at slumber.
No wonder I don't believe.
But the fervent prayers of the righteous
Can surely intercede for me.
If you would just pray for me,
There's a war for my soul

and an enemy I cannot see.
Who wants to strip me from the truth
that Christ died for me.
He appeased me in my youth
that there's nothing to fear,
Not even God who made me …
And to you it's so clear.
I can't feel my soul going down
Or my spirit plunging
to death's bottomless ground.
But you who know
don't watch my death so—lightly.
Pray the scales of my spiritual sight
No longer blind me.
So I can choose to be with the King,
Who can live inside of me.

Intercessor's Responsibility

What a mantle I've placed on you
To intercede for the blue,
For the ones I called forth just like you.
Where once you were a blind transgressor
To now, a big-time believer.

If you do not pray them through,
What fate awaits for my creation,
That does not get my revelation?
I brought them from the East,
West, North and South,
To cross your paths
So you will pray them out.

When they come to you,
Intercede them through
By praising me with your mouth
Of the wonders I will do.
"Oh, yes Lord,
All praises and worship
Goes back to you."

What happened to the little lamb
That didn't believe I AM that I AM?
The one I sent to you,
Who was philosophic,
And called himself an agnostic—
Filled with tricks of the mind
From the enemy that had him blind?

"I don't know, Lord.
For two days I prayed,
But then my thoughts strayed
And I prayed for another soul the next day."

Oh, how bold you say it.
Well, to my dismay, he continued to stray.
Though he may not have, if you continued to pray.
To intercede a few more days as I commanded,
Now his choices reflect the world's view.

If he continues,
He, too, will suffer their fate.
He can be redeemed,
It's not too late.
So please don't grieve me—
It does not please me.
Next time, don't debate,
Do as I command and have faith.

Do not stop praying for my sheep,
The responsibility is beyond deep.
When I wake you from your slumber,
Remember not to blunder.

If you love me,
It's your keep to pray for my sheep.
"Yes, Lord, the meaning is far above me.
I will pray for your sheep
As thou hast commanded me."

I've Been Changed

I need a change in my world,
But nothing happens when my faith stands still.
My faith needs to move and step out,
Moving my mountain and to do His will.
My spirit shouts for change,
But my heart seems stagnant
And circumstances remain the same.
Closed behind the doors of dead works
Does not liberate me first.
It places me last
In a class by myself—*Alone.*
Trying to shake up the foundation of His word in my life
Does not give me liberty, but brings me strife.
Mixing the 'I will' with 'His will'
Gives me freedom of expression,
Knowing that I am moving in the right direction.
I am ready for God to move from His throne,
As I make my intimate prayers to Him known.
Warring for other souls, and for myself as well –
Boldly before His throne.
No one in the world I know can create
His divine love felt in my spirit.
God called me to hear Him,
To manifest His will in my life.
And when He speaks,
I, like sheep to a shepherd, hear it.
I am charged to move out of the way,
So the Holy Spirit can have His way.
There is liberty in my life
When I know where God has brought me from.
He severed the dead things and made all things new.
Starting with my spirit, to which He communicates to.
A renewed mind, well-kept temple,
And tongue that chooses to speak life.

I know I've changed,
It's a matter of growing in love,
Fellowship and calling on His name
Anytime, day or night.
God, you've caused me to see and discern
Where I can now do what's right.
Obediently, my heart bows,
It is humble before you,
And my sacrifice to you renowned.
Thank you, Jesus for sending the Holy Spirit
To bring about so much revelation—so much truth.
It is a good thing to search for Him in your youth.
Let no man get weary finding you,
For you are a rewarder of them
That diligently seek after you.
I believe and know I've changed.
I believe, because of you, Lord,
I will never, ever be the same.
In my life, I may struggle from time to time,
But with you,
I'll run this course knowing you're mine.
I, in you, and you in I,
Like the branch of a vine,
I, perfectly intertwined,
Will abide in you.
If I fall, I will get up and stand,
For in me lives the spirit of the great I AM,
And a kingdom that's at hand.
I am a changed person in you,
For you truly make all things new.

Koo-Koo Bird

The one who flew the koo-koo's nest,
Sometimes cried, sometimes shy,
But gladly, never denied.
May have been ill,
Yet down the road better still, what a thrill.
Went from poppin' seven,
Down to one pill.
Don't skip a day, my doctor prayed.
"I want off this ride, not talkin' pride."
I feel trapped, my mind is capped,
For this was not my beginning.
Coming here is stinging.
My emotions exposed as I write in prose—
Of a time that frowned gray,
A month locked up,
I stayed eating three square meals a day.
Visitors of family, those close to you,
Now life has turned for a loopty loop.
Not for worse, but better of course.
I'm at peace, a feeling of release.
Looking back, I see how God connected me,
I'm free to speak.
The compassion for the mind befuddles me.
To see the beautiful mind and heart,
And tell if it's at peace.
Kindness and love healed me.
His love from up above descended on me,
Like a cool, white dove.
I'm the one who flew the koo-koo's nest,
Who would have guessed?

Needing My Deliverer

I am for Christ dying for me,
Accepted Him as a young lady
At the tender age of twenty-three
Gave my heart to the King.
I was tired of life's trials and stings, like bees
Caught up with the spirits that were familiar to me.
Some supped with my friends,
And never left me—not yet.
I could bet, when I felt like being in a relationship
With a potential mate I would see,
The Spirit of lust jumped all over me.
It bared conceit that I must be seen.

Make way for the spirit of pride –
Less conscience to hide, from inside of me.
Leaving the others behind seemed unnatural to me.
I had to have the spirit of rebellion,
Now that would make three.

Caught up with this familiar pact,
I started to act
Out of my lack of knowledge,
As if Christ did not die for me.
They say I'm saved, but do you really know me?

I would fornicate, then sing on Sunday,
"Holy, Holy, Holy"
For God is Holy, like I needed to be.
After service, these spirits began to suffocate me.
I started to walk out of my purpose.
Oh yes, I know Christ died for me,
But where was the deliverance?
I needed to cast out all three.

I read His Word and prayed all day,
He convicted my soul,
But I needed my Deliverer to deliver me--today.
Cast out lust. I don't want him anymore,
Take out pride that would hide behind closed doors.
I relinquish rebellion that kept my evil deeds score.
This particular one did not take flight without a fight,
I backslid once more.
I went in and out of my church front door.
No one knew about this difficult revolving door.

I watched my grandpa and dad
Drink until they seemed glad.
That bottle of Cognac XO seemed to be all I had.
Drinking until I invited my old friends back
In lust and pride,
Rebellion was open wide,
Legion pushed me down.
At the time, all I could do was cry.
No one knew I already accepted Christ,
And the Lord was on my side.

I had to fast and pray,
Before I was made a grand mockery to His Kingdom.
These familiar spirits thought
They were having a field day,
And sold doubt to me.
It took time, which seemed was not on my side,
I cast them all to the abyss grouped together.
Hell hath no fury as an open scorn made by my God.
What could be better?
I fell out in the spirit, light as a feather.

My house is clean and filled with the Holy Spirit.
I can hardly wait for my family to experience it.
Family curses of the drunken, lust and pride,
Rebelling spirit of rebellion, tagging legion to the side,

No longer has a place in me to hide.
Every minister in place, my deliverance was enacted,
And I live by His love, grace, and tender mercies—
In the Word, prayed up, stayed up,
Warring for my soul and resting in Him,
For I am made whole.

Petting Secret Sins

The secret sins we pet,
The ones we let in,
The ones we know are wrong
To do to us, it is sin.
It jumps on our legs that we stand on,
Begging for a treat,
For you to continue to crave it
Like a delectable piece of meat.

It ropes us in,
Like a juicy, sinful conversation,
Better known as gossip.
When it's all said and done,
We lay low, playing possum.
Waiting for us to feed it,
'Til we come to a place
Where we feel we need it.
It not only locks us in,
It now has a stronghold
And becomes our favorite sin.

No one in the pews seems to know
What we knew,
It's the ones that need to be spewed.
You can't go on living the secret life of sin
You know…the ones that pet your flesh
Deep from within.

Now there's a war in your soul,
Relationship with the Lord
No longer quite whole.
If you're selected from the pew
To confess what you already knew,
Who is to blame

When you're called out to your shame?
Just see to it that you confess and renounce it,
Don't go about lavishly flouncing it,
You must repent for the wicked time spent.

Say, Lord nevertheless,
Please take this sinful way away from me,
This stronghold that I see.
Let me take upon your yoke,
Which is easy, and your burden, which is light.
I'll trust in you, Lord
To make my shortcomings right.

I'm sorry for what I've done,
I want to shine in your presence,
To the glory of your Son.
The only one who died for me,
So that I can be set free
From the enemy that beguiled me,
And whom I've tasted of his soiled meat.

Please forgive me and change my desires
To that which will satisfy my spirit,
Where I can be led by it,
And not of the flesh,
Which would ultimately lead to death.

Give me the life that you have for me,
I am ready to settle this matter.
In you, I know You'll make a way for me.
My former days are minor,
Compared to what You'll have for me
In the latter.

I bless your name for You are true,
I want nothing more than just You, Lord.
My God and the Comforter that You bring.

You make my heart, my mind
And all of my soul sing.

Thank You for your tender mercies and graces,
Your love takes me into the realm of heavenly places.
The sin that was secret has now been exposed,
A harsh lesson learned, has now been brought to a close.

I could have died in my iniquity,
Which was not in the confines of ambiguity.
But knowing full well my intentional sin
Would eventually lead to hell.

For all this, I share
So that you will take care
Of your relationship and walk in Christ,
And not to roll that *seemingly delectable* pair of dice.

The Deadly Seven

The deadly seven sins:
Pride—
Envy—
Wrath—
Sloth—
Lust—
Gluttony
Greed—
The ones that can make your soul burn and bleed.
Learn from them and please take heed.

Pride can hide, as proud as can be,
Making one feel he's above the Creator,
As if man was the one who formed thee and better.
The same God who fashioned Abraham—
Molded Moses—
Identified Isaac—
Stood by Jacob—
And delivered David—
Created you and me.

Humble thyself, 'less you seethe
Burning with wrath
The anger of rage
That would have you locked up in a spiritual cage,
Away from man and the rest of society.
Take on His peace, not the world's propriety,
But His burden, which is light
And His yolk which is easy.

Do not take too much of your selfish desires
How could the Lord trust you to take you higher
And higher in Him?

Surely greed could indeed seep to unholy ties
And selfish desires,
Enough to beckon the saints to pray for you
Reaching higher to God's throne every day.
And spending time with Him like you should
Day by day...

You'll never be alone,
Interceding for your very own soul.
He calls you not to be slothful,
Especially in well doing.
Don't just lay there feeling
The need to stop moving.

God's love brings change,
Which requires you to keep advancing in Him.
Don't be sluggish at best,
For moving in Him, you'll find rest.

Woe to the gluttonous man,
He eats in such excess,
Which all can't be processed,
For comfort, ultimately replacing the Great Comforter.
You see, He wants you to just eat healthy.
Pick up your fork, knife, and spoon,
Just not in excess from your plate,
The Lord is calling you to be healthy
Without the debate.
To stand on guard and not get sick,
Also by the junk food that can be licked.

Do not envy another man's digs, wife, or property,
Or anything that could make you sorry
For wishing that you had it unrightfully.
What is for you, is for you,
Is earned or is blessed to you.
Longing for another man's gift is torture to his soul.

Repent, my friend and be ye whole.
Don't hold it idle in your heart.
He's already blessed you readily from the start
Before you were conceived.
Do not quench the Spirit of God to make Him grieve.

Lust for and of the flesh,
Which our spirit doesn't mesh with the body,
Which craves things that lead to death.
It's the flesh that's at enmity with the spirit nonetheless.
Carried away by our lust,
Is not the full cup of what God has for us.

Satan's plots and schemes,
If accepted, defile our body, spirit, life and dreams.
This is not what God has or wants for us
Even if it seems to be.
He wants us to live our life more abundantly
In the overflow pick up your cross and now go.
Be the light you're called to be
And tell the world of the loving Counselor,
Almighty God you know.
For the seven can leaven
In our soul and are indeed deadly,
That goes for all that's righteous and ungodly.
Just stay the course of your salvation,
I say again, be the light and strengthen your brethren.

Two of a Kind

God created Adam and Eve,
Not for man and man to take the stand
And receive in himself the error of his ways
For the rest of his days.
Nor for a woman to lay with a woman and
Act as uncomely and ungodly,
Which is to be judged by God only.
But to create—
You and me to procreate,
To subdue this great place called earth,
The fish of the sea, the birds in the trees.
Change your ways same sex mate.
Submit your will to the Great One.
Whose love is great and undefiled by no means,
You feel right, you say,
You think it's okay to be gay?
I cry with all my might,
It is wrong in God's sight.
There is deliverance just for you.
When God created man He made two of a kind,
Don't be blind.
Don't turn His creations into worldly abominations,
There is gestation in all nations.
Don't go with how you feel,
That's how the devil deals.
You are a precious soul to Him,
Don't paint your picture grim.
He loves you!
He loves you, not your sin!

What is Your Idol?

So idle with idols,
What's your fix in the mix
That's betwixt you and the Lord?
Is it your time when you gored on food
Instead of His daily bread?

Is it your itchy ears for gossip,
When you need Him instead,
To minister a word to you from time to time?
Is it your phone with all those apps,
When you need to lean on Him and adapt,
To these changing times?

I center myself in Him
When I know I need to praise Him,
And let Him know He's mine
With all my heart, soul and mind,
To give the Lord quality time.

Who or what's your idol when your temple, your body,
should be bridled to His heart's desires?
How can He take you higher and higher,
When you should inquire of Him more and explore.

Cast away all idols which craftily cut away
His time with you
When all He wants to reveal
Is His will and truth to you,
And give you the desires of your heart.
As long as you don't ask amiss,
Or betray Him with a kiss,
Making unnecessary requests and demands,
When it's His Kingdom that's at hand.
No idols, please!

Allow your spirit to go on its knees
Before me and you will see,
Those dumb idols have no place in me.
When I died for you, hung on that tree.

You will see,
When you toss your idols and say,
"I do love thee single-heartedly,
The Christ you've placed in me."
I am your Rock.
Those idols will block you from Me.
Open your spirit man loud,
Where it can be heard unto the Holy Trinity,
Come taste and see the goodness of the Lord,
Let us now be on one accord.

Your Temple - A Home

Walk away from lust and cussing,
Lies and cheating, beating wives,
Dope and coke,
Dragging out that one last smoke.

Fornicating 'til the cows come home,
Hanging out with riff raff,
Abusing yourself,
Making your body an unholy home.

Give the Holy Spirit
Rest in a clean temple
So He can operate at best,
Calling your soul to God's test.

Pick up your cross,
Let Christ in you walk out the rest.
Follow Him on your quest.
Then my friend,
Your soul can truly rest.

'Til death do you part?
Not even *that* can separate you
From the heart of God.

A Call to Salvation
and Repentance

Everyone has a past. Many may recognize they are in need of a Savior for we have all fallen short of the glory of God. Being a good person does not give you a ticket to heaven. Receiving what Jesus Christ did on the cross by faith is the way to salvation.

John 3:16 KJV says, "For God so loved the world that he gave his only Begotten Son, that whosoever believeth in him should not perish, but have everlasting life."

We all need the Savior. That Savior is Jesus Christ. Some recognize it and some do not. By no other means is a person saved. Jesus is that Savior. He can be that for you today, right here, right now. The Word of God (The Bible) says that Jesus who was without sin became sin, was made the sacrifice so that those who received his death on the cross for our sins may be saved by faith. "For he hath made him to be sin for us, who knew no sin, that we might be made the righteousness of God in him" (2 Corinthians 5:21 KJV).

"For by grace are ye saved through faith, and that not yourselves: *it is* the gift of God: not of works, lest any man boast" (Ephesians 2:8-9 KJV).

Acts 4:12 KJV says, "Neither is there salvation in any other: for there is none other name under heaven given among men, whereby we must be saved."

Romans 10:9-10 KJV says, "that if thou shalt confess with thy mouth, the Lord Jesus, and shalt believe in thine heart that God hath raised him from the dead, thou shalt be saved. For with the heart man believeth unto righteousness, and with the mouth confession is made unto salvation."

God is not willing that any man perish but that all come unto repentance.

"The Lord is not slack concerning his promise, as some men count slackness, but is longsuffering to usward, not willing that any should perish, but that all should come to repentance" (2 Peter 3:9 KJV).

John 14:6 KJV says, "Jesus saith unto him, I am the way, the truth, and the life: no man cometh unto the Father, but by me." If you are willing to be saved, or wish to rededicate your life to Jesus Christ, just say...

Lord Jesus, I know I am a sinner. I ask that you forgive me. Please come into my heart and wash me clean. I believe by faith that you who were without sin died on the cross for my transgressions and rose on the third day that I may be saved, healed, delivered, and set free. I want to start a new life in you. I thank you. Teach me your ways, Lord. Help me walk upright before you.

It's that simple. You are saved. Hallelujah! The angels of God are cheering for you and I'm cheering for you too. Know that it is not in your own strength, but through Christ who strengthens us. Philippians 4:13 KJV says, "I can do all things through Christ which strengthened me."

Welcome into the Kingdom of God. Your journey in the Lord is a process. Find a good Bible-based teaching church and allow God to process you layer by layer. It may not always be easy but it will certainly be worth it.

Next, reading your Bible and allowing the Holy Spirit to lead, teach, and guide you is important. Pray and listen. Talk to the Lord like you would your friend. He is the best friend you will EVER have. The Father, Jesus, and the Holy Spirit, will help you navigate this thing called life.

I now pronounce a blessing over you.
"May the Lord bless thee and keep thee: The Lord make his face shine upon thee, and be gracious unto thee: The Lord lift up his countenance upon thee, and give thee peace (Numbers 6:24-26 KJV).

Works Cited

Deliverance. *Dictionary.com.* Dictionary.com, LLC.
www.dictionary.com/browse/deliverance.
Accessed May 2022.

Heber, Reginald, "Holy, Holy, Holy". All-American
Church Hymnal, Composer Dykes, John B.,
Eleventh Edition, John T. Benson, Jr. Publisher,
1957, p. 115.

Holy Bible. King James Version. Large Print Compact
Edition, Nashville, Tn, Holman Bible Publishers,
2000.

Hope. *Dictionary.com*, Dictionary.com, LLC,
www.dictionary.com/browse/hope. Accessed
May 2022.

Holy Bible Inspire Edition. New Living Translation,
Tyndale House Publishers Inc., Carol Stream,
Ill., 2015.

King James Version. Bible Gateway,
www.biblegateway.com. Accessed 24 August
2022.

Love. *Dictionary.com*, Dictionary.com, LLC,
www.dictionary.com/browse/love. Accessed
May 2022.

Praise. *Dictionary.com*, Dictionary.com. LLC,
www.dictionary.com/browse/praise. Accessed
May 2022.

Salvation. *Dictionary.com*, Dictionary.com, LLC, www.dictionary.com/browse/salvation. Accessed May 2022.

Worship. *Dictionary.com*, Dictionary.com, LLC, www.dictionary.com/browse/worship. Accessed May 2022.

About Hazel O. Kersellius

 Hazel O. Kersellius, a Guyanese American, was born on a U.S. military base to Guyanese parents in Nuremberg, Germany. Relocating to the South as a young girl, she has lived most of her teenage and adult years in New York City.

A devout, born-again Christian who believes in the power of God through the Lord Jesus Christ, Kersellius submitted her life to the Lord and was baptized at the renowned Brooklyn Tabernacle in 2010.

Kersellius has a prophetic call on her life, accompanied with a desire for souls to be saved. With an innate passion for writing Christian poetry for more than a decade, she uses her spiritual gift of writing to encourage others to seek Christ by having a personal relationship with the Lord.

Kersellius is an active member at Saint Albans Gospel Assembly, Queens, New York where she serves as a part of a special women's prison ministry. She attended Brooklyn College, C.U.N.Y. in Brooklyn, New York and graduated with a Broadcast Journalism degree. She hopes to inspire people to seek God and give Him first place in their life.

Kersellius works diligently to uplift and encourage the hearts of God's people through her creative writing. She is often invited to churches, assemblies, and secular venues to minister God's love through her poetry.

"Expressions for the Lover of My Soul" is Kersellius' first book. It is the author's hope that you will find joy, solace, peace, healing and deliverance through her poetic works and that it will lead you to foster a closer relationship with the Lord, or start one if you have not already done so.

To arrange speaking engagements, book signings, festival/conference attendance and/or to purchase personal autographed copies of this book, contact the author Hazel O. Kersellius at hazelexpressions@gmail.com